Alfred James Waterhouse

Some Homely Little Songs

Alfred James Waterhouse

Some Homely Little Songs

ISBN/EAN: 9783744767231

Printed in Europe, USA, Canada, Australia, Japan

Cover: Foto ©Andreas Hilbeck / pixelio.de

More available books at **www.hansebooks.com**

.. SOME ..

HOMELY LITTLE SONGS

.. BY ..

ALFRED JAMES WATERHOUSE

SAN FRANCISCO

THE WHITAKER & RAY CO.

(INCORPORATED)

1899

To one whose love has never varied—my mother—this book of Homely Little Songs is dedicated.

INDEX.

Some Homely Little Songs.

WHEN BABY PRAYS.

WHEN baby by her crib at night
 Enfolds her little hands to pray—
Dear little hands so soft and white,—
 I listen while the sweet lips say:
  " Now I 'ay me down to s'eep,
  I p'ay the Lord my soul to teep;"
And, listening, years are backward rolled;
The past is as a tale untold.

And, standing by my mother mild—
 Dear mother, with your hair of white—
Again I am a little child,
 And say again, as yester night:
  " If I s'ould die before I wate,
  I pa'y the Lord my soul to tate;"
And half it seems in baby's plea
The olden faith comes back to me.

Ah me! I know my faith is but
  A phantom of the long ago;
Yet, when my babe, with eyelids shut,
  Repeats the words I used to know:
    " Now I 'ay me down to s'eep,
    I p'ay the Lord my soul to teep,"
Someway, someway, the world-doubts flee;
The old, sweet faith comes back to me.

It comes again, the old, sweet faith;
  It is my own, it is my own,
And doubt has fled, the gloomy wraith,
  Before a baby's words alone:
    " If I s'ould die before I wate,
    I p'ay the Lord my soul to tate."
So, for a baby's lisping plea,
My thanks, dear Lord, my thanks to Thee.

BUNNER OF 'FRISCO.

BUNNER of 'Frisco—knew him well;
　　Queer little chap as ever you met;
Always insistin' that war was hell—
　"Regular Hades it is, you bet."
When there resounded the call "To Arms!"
　　Bunner of 'Frisco was first to go;
Sailed to the field of death and alarms,
　　Always remarkin', "It's hell, you know."

Bunner of 'Frisco—once a squad
　　Got where the "gugus" were fifty to one.
Wholly surrounded, their summons to God
　　Came with each crack of a savage's gun.
"Boys," said the sergeant, "one, you know,
　　Must go to the captain our case to tell.
Probably death for him—who will go?"
　　"I will," says Bunner, "but war is hell."

Bunner of 'Frisco—up the hill,
　　While demons yelled, and over its crest;
And the bullets sung, and their song was shrill—
　　Now, Bunner of 'Frisco, now do your best!

He did it, by Heaven ! On and on,
  Into the river where missiles hailed;
Wounded and staggering, growing wan,
  Never a moment he halted or quailed.

Bunner of 'Frisco—into the camp,
  Gory and dying, he staggered, they say,
Wiped from his forehead the ultimate damp,
  Delivered his message and fainted away.
He spoke once again: "The boys will be
    saved"—
  Slowly the words from his ashen lips fell;
Turned his dim eyes to where the flag waved—
  "The boys will be saved, but—war—war is—
    hell."

          *   *   *   *   *

Bunner of 'Frisco, I don't know
  Whither you journey, or where you drift,
Past where the life-tides ebb and flow,
  There where the waves of Eternity shift;
But one thing I know, or I think I do,
  You followed your duty through pain and woe,
And I judge, in the place that was kept for you,
  You never will murmur, " It's hell, you know."

HE DRIFTED.

H E drifted along on the river of life—
       Just drifted
When the current grew sullen, and weary the
      strife,
              He shifted.
He would sit on a box in the glint o' the sun
An' whittle up sticks around, one after one.
With plenty to do an' with little yet done,
              He drifted.

With a talent for restin' this ease-takin' man
              Was gifted,
Though he'd fish from a bank where a slow river
      ran,
              Or shifted.
For he said that to labor was too much like
      work,
An' he guessed he could live and the hard strug-
      gles shirk,
An' he 'lowed that old Fortune's best smile is a
      smirk—
              So he drifted.

When the messenger came and beckoned him on
                He drifted
Through the door in the mist which the death
        angel wan
                Uplifted;
An' if he reached Heaven I'm here to suggest
In the shade of the throne he is takin' a rest,
An' wonderin' if harp-bangin' can't be sup-
        pressed
                Where he's drifted.

NOW, WHY WAS THIS?

WHEN the baby came he was homely as sin,
 With a very bald pate and a very weak
  chin,
With gums that were toothless and watery eyes,
A nose like a blur and a talent for cries;
And the women all said as he wriggled and
  scowled
And puckered and twisted and bellowed and
  howled—
They said as they viewed him with critical eye:
" He's just like his father. Now, isn't he? My!
   Why-y-y!
You can see the resemblance with half of an eye."

As the baby grew he was ugly some days,
With a strong inclination a hubbub to raise;
That his temper was grievous was plain to be
  seen,
And with squalling and bawling he kept himself
  lean.

He howled till his mouth wore a permanent
    twist,
And the pleasure of living he constantly missed;
And when he yelled loudest the women would
    cry:
" He favors his father. Now, doesn't he? My!
        Why-y-y!
You can see the resemblance with half of an eye."

But a change was seen as the baby grew,
For his looks improved and his temper, too,
And his smiles chased the frowns and the scowls
    away,
And the sunbeams loved in his dimples to play;
And I thought him sweet, in my fatherly pride,
As he toddled along on the floor at my side;
And then all the women who saw him would cry:
" He's just like his mother. Now, isn't he? My!
        Why-y-y!
You can see the resemblance with half of an eye."

WHEN THE BABY DIED.

WHEN the baby died, so fair was she—
Like a lily an angel had dropped for me—
That I said to myself: " She is only asleep,"
And I wondered that others would over her
weep;
And I stooped and kissed her, half dreaming she
Would open her blue eyes unto me,
And laugh again as on yesterday,
And dimple and croon in the dear old way—
When the baby died.

When the baby died I could not weep,
And I said: " She is only asleep—asleep.
She will wake ere long and I shall hear
The prattle I love beat on my ear."
And I smoothed all gently the golden hair,
And I would not believe she was otherwhere
As I cried, " My darling, look up and see!"
But only the night wind answered me—
When the baby died.

When the baby died—sometimes I start
From a dream at night with a longing heart,
For I fancy I hear through the silence wide
A prattle of words from the babe that died.
Then my hands fall down, though they empty be,
For I know that my darling has gone from me,
And the night creeps into a somber day,
While my heart cries out: "Come back, I
    pray"—
        Since the baby died.

NIGHTTIME IN CALIFORNIA.

N IGHTTIME in California. There's noth-
　　ing like it found,
Though to and fro you come and go and journey
　　earth around.
The skies are like a crystal sea, with islands made
　　of stars;
The moon's a fairy ship that sails among its
　　shoals and bars;
And on that sea I sit and look, and wonder
　　where it ends;
If I shall sail its phantom wave, and where the
　　journey tends,
And if—in vain I wonder; let's change the sol-
　　emn theme,
For the nights of California were made for man
　　to dream.

Nighttime in California. The cricket's note is
    heard,
And now, perhaps, the twitter of a drowsy,
    dreaming bird.
An oar is plashing yonder; the wakeful frogs re-
    ply.
The breeze is chanting in the trees a ghostly lull-
    aby.
The moon has touched with silver the peaceful,
    sleeping world,
And in the weary soul of man the flag of sor-
    row's furled.
'Tis a time for smiles and music; 'tis a time for
    love divine,
For the nights of California are Heav'n this side
    the line.

Nighttime in California. Elsewhere men only
    guess
At the glory of the evenings that are perfect—
    nothing less;
But here the nights, returning, are the wondrous
    gifts of God—
As if the days were maidens fair with golden slip-
    pers shod.
There is no cloud to hide the sky; the universe is
    ours,
And the starlight likes to look and laugh in Cu-
    pid-haunted bowers.
Oh, the restful, peaceful evenings! In them my
    soul delights,
For God loved California when He gave to her
    her nights.

O'ER THE SEA OF DREAMS.

O'ER the sea of dreams to the sweet Dream-
    land—
Oh, little my love, come hither, I pray,
And place in my own your wee white hand
    And we will go sailing away, away,
Down a path of gold by the Isles of Rest,
    O'er the slumbrous depths of the Sundown
        Sea,
To the land of lands that we love the best,
    Where dream angels whisper to you and to me.

O'er the sea of dreams—oh, little my love,
    Closer yet creep to this heart of mine,
While lowly the dream angels hover above
    And there in God's meadows the star-blossoms
        shine.
Under your eyelids the visions shall creep.
    Little one, little one, what shall they be?
Something to cause you to smile in your sleep,
    Nestling yet closer and closer to me.

O'er the sea of dreams to the sweet Dreamland—
  Oh, little my love, what dreams they must be,
Such dreams as a baby may understand,
  Queer little fancies, as all must agree,
Little half notions, or foolish or wise,
  Wee floating fragments of babyhood lore;
These are your dreams, as I sagely surmise—
  Heigh-ho, my little one, what are mine more?

O'er the sea of dreams; and who's at the helm,
  Oh, little my love, nor you nor I
May wisely tell, for the sleep king's realm
  Is hidden by mists from the passers-by.
It is hidden by mists, yet myself I tell,
  While your eyelids flutter like petals of white:
The One who is guiding will guide her well—
  So, little my love, good night, good night.

WHEN I WENT OUT A-HARVESTING.

IT'S well enough to talk about the joys the
    farmers know—
Perhaps 'twill sort of brace them up to grapple
    with their woe;
It's well to sing a pæan to the sturdy sons of
    toil
Who labor 'neath a summer sun and boil and
    broil and boil;
But you'll kindly please to notice I'm not joining
    in the strain,
For my farming recollections bring to me a
    sense of pain,
And the horny-handed granger's life to me is
    lacking charm
Since I went out a-harvesting on Deacon Big-
    gins' farm.

I was young and somewhat hopeful, and the deacon said he'd pay
A dollar for my services on any blessed day.
So I went to labor for him. The recollection
still
Of what ensued is haunting me; I judge it ever
will.
For when the deacon called me in the morn at
half past three
To rustle out and do the chores, it was a shock
to me;
And I longed to kill the cattle or to do them
other harm,
When I went out a-harvesting on Deacon Big-
gins' farm.

At half past five was breakfast, and then came
family prayers.
I still recall the good man's words, 'mid all life's
cumbering cares:
"We praise Thee, Lord," he murmured, "for
Thy mercy's constant streams—
Now, boys, get out and hustle till you've hitched
up all the teams."

And we got out and hustled, and the words we
    bandied there,
While hitching up the weary teams, were not the
    words of prayer,
For we judged the deacon's righteousness would
    keep us from all harm,
When I went out a-harvesting on Deacon Big-
    gins' farm.

Oh, days of weary labor by an awful hotness hit!
Did I enjoy a farmer's bliss?   Well, I am doubt-
    ing it.
From half past three of mornings till ten o'clock
    of nights,
We toiled and broiled and broiled and toiled and
    knew the farm's delights;
And still at times I hear these words and wake
    from restless dreams:
" We praise Thee for Thy mercy and—now hus-
    tle out the teams."
And so I am not singing in praise of farming's
    charm,
Since I went out a-harvesting on Deacon Big-
    gins' farm.

ARCADY.

" OUT yonder," she would say to me,
   " Lies Heaven-land, lies Arcady.
Just yonder where the blue skies drop
Beyond the distant mountain's top,
The valley lies where all are blest;
The land of love and peace and rest.
Oh, let us go," she said to me,
" And find that land of Arcady."

And so we wandered hand in hand
To find that peaceful, happy land;
(Ah, that was years, long years ago,
And we were dreamers well I know),
But though we wandered long and far,
From morning star to evening star,
Yet did the happy vision flee;
We found not lovely Arcady.

And then she wearied on the way,
More wistful grew her eyes of gray.
(Ah, dark, sad day of long ago,
How did my tears unceasing flow!)
One long, long kiss—one last embrace—
The Angel's message on her face,
And then she passed from life and me
And found, I know, her Arcady.

Since then, I've wandered far and long,
Have seen the world and met its wrong;
I've sought in vain the land of peace,
The land where care and trouble cease.
'Twas but the vision of our youth—
The years have taught their bitter truth—
Yet still in dreams she whispers me,
" We'll meet and love in Arcady."

LO, I AM THE CHANGELESS.

L O, I am the Changeless, the Deathless.
    Lo, I am the Passionless, Still.
In my presence archangels are breathless,
    And the universe throbs at my will.
I wait, and the ages flit by me.
    I wait, and their story is told.
All of life and of death hovers nigh me,
    And I am the New and the Old.

In the dust of their definite places
    My atoms, my men, they plod on;
And they lift to the heavens their faces,
    Their faces all troubled and wan;
And they dream, and they term their dream,
        living;
    They dream, and their dream is, to die:
They dream they are gaining or giving—
    And over them, changeless, am I.

They dream of the glitter of treasure—
  I shatter the dream at my will.
They dance to the rhythm of pleasure—
  I nod, and the dancers are still.
They dream of the glory of power,
  My atomies born for a day.
Ay, the visions press fast for an hour—
  I nod, and the dreamers obey.

Lo, I am the Changeless, the Deathless.
  All other shall blossom and fade.
I speak, and the ages are breathless,
  And the drama of living is played.
And whether the sleepers shall waken,
  Or whether they dream as they lie,
Unheeding, uncaring, unshaken,
  None other may answer save I.

WHEN PA FIRS' ET TABASCO SAUCE.

WHEN pa firs' et tabasco sauce—I'm smilin' 'bout it yet,
Although his subsekent remarks I always shall
regret.
We'd come to town to see the sights, an' pa remarked to me:
"We'll eat at a bong tong hotel an' sling some
style," says he.
An' then he sort o' cast his eye among the plates
an' all,
An' says, "That ketchup mus' be good; the bot-
tle is so small;"
An' then he took a piece of meat an' covered it
quite thick,
When pa firs' et tabasco sauce an' rose to make
his kick.

It all comes back so plain to me; I rikollect it
    well;
He just was talkin' mild an' calm, an' then he
    give a yell
An' tried to cave the ceilin' in by buttin' with his
    head.
" Er-hooh! Er-hooh! Fire! Murder! Hooh! " I
    can't tell all he said,
But when they heard his heated words six wo-
    men lef' the room
An' said such language filled their souls with
    shame an' also gloom,
But pa he only gurgled some, an' then he yelled
    again,
When firs' he et tabasco sauce an' told about it
    then.

We laid him out upon a board an' fanned him
    quite a while,
An' pa he sort o' gasped at firs' an' then he tried
    to smile,
An' says: " Jus' heat a poker now an' run it
    down my neck—
I want to cool off gradual; it's better, I expeck."

But when he got me out o' doors, he says: " I
    want to get
Thet there blame ketchup's recipe an' learn jes'
    how it's het,
So I can try it on the boys when you an' me git
    hum,
Till they, too, think the condiment is mixed with
    Kingdom Come."

I've told the story, but I guess perhaps I
    oughtn't to,
Fer pa don't go with me no more, the way he
    used to do.
He said some words, of course I know, that were
    too sizzlin' hot,
But still I hope up where he's gone they're all of
    them forgot.
An' if they ain't per'aps my pa will to the an-
    gels say:
" I wish you'd try that ketchup stuff I et down
    there that day."
Of course I feel they can't approve, but I hope,
    just the same,
If once they eat tabasco sauce they'll count him
    less to blame.

WHEN UNCLE JABEZ COME.

WHEN Uncle Jabez come to see my folks
    an' me out here,
Where California's summers keep a-lingerin'
    through the year,
He kind o' took one look around, an' then he
    says, " Amen "—
The poppies shone like fields of gold—he whis-
    pered it again;
An' when I asked him why, he says: " Sech
    glory everywhere!
Yew knew, my boy, it seems tew me jest like
    ole natur's prayer;"
And then he kind o' sighed, an' says: " I wish
    yew'd tell, I vum,
Just haow yew folks what's livin' here can tell
    when winter's come."

I showed him where the mountains glow like
    fields by angels trod,
An' how the rose keeps smilin' back unto the
    smile o' God,
An' how the rivers sparkle on without no ice to
    chill,
An' how the birds with all their songs keep na-
    ture all a-thrill;
An' he, he just stood there and breathed as
    though the air was dear,
An' says: " Ef this is heaven—well, say haow
    did I git here?
We don't hev things like this back East; it ain't
    the same tew hum.
Haow in tarnation dew yew tell when winter
    time hes come?"

I showed him pumpkins overgrown. He looked,
    an' says: " B' gosh,
Yew call that thing a punkin here? Back hum
    we call it squash."
An' where the orange hides its gold behind a
    screen of green
He looked, an' sighed, an' softly said: " Ef
    mother could o' seen!"

An' then he brushed a tear away—she died not
    long ago—
An' the mockin' bird was whistlin' a tender song,
    an' low;
An' then he sort o' straightened up, an' says,
    says he: " I vum,
I can't see haow yew people know when winter
    time hes come."

So Uncle Jabez, he's arranged to stay out here,
    you know;
He says he kind o' calkerlates 'twill make him
    younger grow
To live awhile where man is close to nature's
    lovin' heart
An' God A'mighty an' His child is not so far
    apart;
An' then he says: " An' ef I die, the diff'rence
    will be small;
Tew go from here tew Heav'n I guess won't be
    no jump at all."
But when we're all alone he says: " I vaow, I'm
    puzzled some
Tew calkerlate how I can tell jest when the win-
    ter's come."

"I PLEAD THY LOVE."

IF I should go to-night where One doth sit
  Upon a great and white and awful throne;
If back from me the mists of time should flit,
  Leaving my soul and me to stand alone
In that vast presence, and if He should say:
  "What is thy plea, poor soul, for peace
    above?"
I would not then, despairing, turn away,
  But low would answer: "Lord, I plead Thy
    love."

I could not plead my merit. Nay, my way
  Is strewn with wrack of faith and hope and
    trust.
Life's dawn broke golden, but its eve grows
    gray,
  And sin has turned its flowers to yellow dust.
Yet, as a wayward child turns home at night,
  Trusting the love all other loves above,
So will I turn, well knowing all is right,
  As low I whisper: "Lord, I plead Thy love."

HOW THE FLOWERS GROW.

DO you know, darling, how pansies grow?
God takes the tints of the sunset glow,
The purple that floats in the mountain mist,
The blush of a maid by her love first kissed,
The blue that's asleep in the midday skies,
The brown that I love in my baby's eyes,
And He mingles them all in a flower; and so,
That is the way that the pansies grow.

Do you know, darling, how lilies grow?
God takes the soul of the beautiful snow
And molds it into a chalice sweet,
Pure and wonderful, fair, complete;
Then He takes the gold of my baby's hair
And sets it amid the whiteness there,
As in night's white skies the bright stars glow;
And that is the way that the lilies grow.

Do you know, darling, how roses grow?
Ah, that is the strangest of all, I know;
For they are the fairest of all things fair,
The one perfect blossom, beyond compare;
Symbol of sweetness and all loveliness—
God wished His children to comfort and bless,
And He wrote the thought in a flower; and so,
That is the way that the roses grow.

HEY THERE, LITTLE GIRLS.

HEY there, little girls, who live in the West,
And were born here, you know, 'cause you
thought it was best,
Have you ever heard tell of the wonderful East,
Where the frost makes of little girls' noses a
feast,
Where the snowbirds wear stockings to warm
their poor toes,
And perhaps it's your finger, perhaps it's your
nose
That is frozen, you know,
And your tears won't flow,
For they freeze into ice in your eyes? Oh! Oh!
Have you ever heard tell?
You haven't? Well! Well!
Now listen to me, and you'll know, know, know.

Hey there, little girls, you'll be 'stonished to
    know
That back in the East the rain is just snow;
And the poor little kitties all have to wear fur,
And their breath freezes hard whenever they
    purr,
And if the dogs bark, that bark it will freeze,
And they use it, you know, to cover the trees,
        And instead of " Hello!"
        Meeting, folks say, " I know
That my ears both are frozen; they're frozen.
    Oh! Oh!"
        Had you ever heard tell?
        You hadn't? Well! Well!
It really is time you should know, know, know.

Hey there, little girls, have you ever heard tell
How they hang their thermometers out in the
    well,
And the mercury drops, and it drops, and it
    drops,
'Till it reaches the water, and that's where it
    stops;

And they thaw little girls—it's a terrible shock!—
And melt them each day at just four o'clock.
> And the chilblains, you know,
> They bite at your toe
Till it itches, and itches, and itches? Oh! Oh!
> Did you ever hear tell?
> You didn't? Well! Well!
I'm really so glad now you know, know, know.

Hey there, little girls; the cyclones blow there,
And they take little children right up in the air,
And they twist them and whirl them around and
    around
Till their papas don't know them, supposing
    they're found;
And sometimes they blow them clear up to the
    sky,
And they never come back again! Never! Oh, my!
> Would you like East to go?
> You wouldn't, I know,
For I've tried it myself, and it's dreadful. Oh! Oh!
> So you hadn't heard tell?
> You hadn't? Well! Well!
It was certainly time you should know, know,
    know.

THE TEACHER KNOWS.

ONE time my teacher said, says she:
" It's no use talkin'; seems to me
That you're the worst boy that I've got;
You're worser than the rest, a lot.
I've whipped you, an' I've scolded, too;
Don't make no difference what I do;
You keep right on jus' if I'd not.
Ain't you the worst boy that I've got? "

An' then my teacher said, says she:
" Your case is always puzzlin' me.
Now don't you know it hurts me, too,
When scoldin' or a whippin' you?
I always want you to be good
 An' actin' like a nice boy should,
Because I love you "—Then she sighed,
An' I—I—well, I up an' cried.

Since then my teacher's gone away,
An' I don't go to school an' play
An' study some, 's I used to do
Before my schoolin' days was through.
But still my Teacher says, says He:
" I'm teachin' you as seems to me
Is best; with sorrow's sting an' blow
I'm teachin' you the way to go."

An' then my Teacher says, says He:
" If only you'll look up to me
Through eyes bedimmed with trouble's rain,
You'll learn the lesson hid in pain,
An' know, though cruel seems the blow,
'Twas dealt because I love you so."
An', though I'm weary an' oppressed,
I guess my Teacher knows the best.

SWING LOW, STARS.

SWING low, stars, for I want to hear your
    singing.
  I want to hear the slumber song you murmur
    to the night
In the distant, distant spaces where an angel
    host is winging
  Its way between the moonbeams to the farther
    fields of light.
The daytime has its voices, but a cry is ringing
    through them,
  The weary cry of sorrow, the cruel cry of
    wrong,
And we look upon God's sunlight in anguish to
    renew them—
  Swing low, stars, for I want to hear your song.

Sleep—sleep—
Sleep—sleep;
Better dream than wake to weep.
Care and doubt
May mortals flout
When the stars, the stars creep out.

Swing low, stars, for I've been dreaming, dream-
    ing
  That up above the crystal heights is peace and
    always peace,
And I'm burdened by the toiling, and I'm weary
    of the scheming,
  And I'd like to find a country where the care
    and labor cease.
The days are full of effort, but the tranquil nights
    are tender
  As the eyes of one who loved me well, oh, long
    ago, so long;
So I turn from pain and passion to the nights of
    peaceful splendor—
  Swing low, stars, for I want to hear your song.

        Rest—rest—
        Children, rest;
    Care is but a daytime guest.
        None should weep—
        Children, sleep—
    While the stars their vigils keep.

WHEN MOTHER CALLED.

M OTHER used to come and say:
  " Come, little boy, it's time to rise.
Wake right up, without delay;
  Shake yourself and rub your eyes."
An' I'd say: " Huh! Wha—Ye-e-es," and then—
  · Go right off to sleep again.

After while she'd come and say,
  Just as gently as before:
" Wake and see this lovely day.
  Don't go to sleep, dear, any more."
An' I'd say: " Yes—I'm—coming; " then—
  Go right off to sleep again.

Didn't matter though; no less
  Patient, gentle, kind was she
When she came and said: " I guess
  My little boy asleep must be."
An' I said: " I'll—get—up," and then—
  Went right off to sleep again.

Then my grandpa came to call.
  'Twas but little that he said;
Just one word, and that was all,
  Just one word, and that, " Al-*fred !* "
Just one word, you see, but then—
    I didn't go to sleep again.

Just that difference! But, you see,
  I've been thinking here alone,
Should my mother now call me
  In the tender, gentle tone
Of the past, I'd wake, and then—
    I wouldn't go to sleep again.

TWO PRAYERS.

GREAT God, 'tis not for soul or heart
    I plead with thee;
Nor that I act a nobler part,
    Or better be;
'Tis not that I erect may stand
    While life-dreams crash,
Nor that I reach a helping hand,
    But just for cash.

Lord, give me cash; I fain would be
    Like all the rest;
No other god than red gold see,
    But hold it best.
I'd barter honor, virtue, good
    That life may hold,
And make my higher nature's food
    Just gold—gold—gold.

The sorry sting of other's pain
    I would not know,
For callous hearts may hope for gain
    In coin; and so
I'd bury sympathy for all
    And hug myself,
Engrossed in my ambitions small,
    My greed for pelf.

So, Father, kill my better part
    That I may be
Devoid of feeling and of heart
    As those I see
About me, callous to the woe
    That hems them in;
Let me no care for others know,
    But lucre win.

I knew a millionaire, and he
    Was praised of men;
O'er petty, small, he seemed to me,
    And base, but then,
He had his gold and people bowed,
    Or feared his lash.
I'd have the plaudits of the crowd,
    So give me cash.

      *   *   *   *   *

So runs the prayer. But 'tis not mine—
    Dear God, forbid!
For I have felt Thy thought divine
    In me is hid;
I know that o'er the petty throng
    There stands Thy Truth,
The principle that combats wrong,
    Dream of my youth.

It stands unmoved. Our little lives
    Wail out their song;
Ill-seeming greed in fatness thrives,
    But not for long;
For still Thy Truth moves changeless on
    Through time's long day,
And still shall rule when stars grow wan—
    Show me Thy way.

SAVE YOUR LETTERS.

SEE here, you little fellows, whom I cannot
  help but like,
Why don't you save your letters, and so get
  yourselves a bike ?
Or if you do not know the way, or think I talk
  in fun,
If you'll listen for a moment, I will tell you how
  it's done:

Spell "rubber" r-u-b-e-r, and there you save a
  • "b,"
And that's a letter that you need, as any one can
  see.
Then next spell "lief" just l-e-f, and I've no
  doubt you'll like
To notice that you now have saved b-i, one-half
  of bike.

And then spell " stick " s-t-i-c; you've saved a
" k," you see,
And b-i-k is not so bad; it only lacks an " e;"
And we know how to save an " e;" we'll take the
small word " dike "
And spell it simply d-i-k, and there! You have
your bike!

So now, my little fellows, whom I could not fail
to like,
Start in to save your letters, and so get yourselves a bike.
And, if your ingenuity is not exceeding small,
I think, no doubt, you, too, can save some marbles and a ball.

IT'S CHRISTMAS TIME.

IT'S Christmas time; it's Christmas time.
Let Christmas bells ring out their chime;
Let Christmas fairies trip along,
A merry, maddening, gladdening throng;
Let Christmas blessings bring their bliss;
Let Christmas angels stoop and kiss
The world's gray heart to tuneful rhyme,
For, oh, it's Christmas, Christmas time.

It's Christmas time, both East and West,
But there the earth is crystal dressed,
While here its robes are bonnie green,
With brooks as silver threads between.
Cold winter there, bright winter here;
For them the frost, for us the cheer;
But East or West, to live's sublime
In merry, merry Christmas time.

In Christmas time, or far or near,
There's just one creed: Be of good cheer.
There's just one song that rings again:
Peace, peace on earth; good will to men.
On this one day let's care forget,
The grief we know, the ill we met,
And let the bells ring chime on chime,
In Christmas time, the merry time.

"HIS LIFE A FAILURE."

H E had no " business tact;" 'tis plain enough.
      He stored no gold while on his earthly
            way;
Ill clad was he, with garments worn and rough;
   Scarce knowing how he'd live from day to day.
Improvident! His little all he gave
   To those who needed; poor, yet fed the poor,
And still neglected for himself to save.
   Unhoused, unkempt, they voted him a boor—
         No tact had he!

No wisdom, surely! Why, the vagrant dared
   To lift his voice 'gainst rulers of the State.
Not e'en the church — God save us all! — he
      spared,
   But scourged alike earth's sainted and her
      great.
To save a sinner, he, unwise, would say
   That you must touch him with a tender hand;
Must touch the wretch of coarser, baser clay!
   Say, when was e'er a scheme so foolish
      planned?
         No wisdom his!

Fanatic, too! He held a strange belief
  That man might reach to heights as yet but
    guessed;
And, hoping much, he walked a path of grief
  That théy who falter might the more be
    blessed.
Aye, thus he dreamed; who doubts the dream
    was vain?
  And thus he lived; was e'er such folly known?
Why, when he died, still scouting golden gain,
  His grave was bought by charity alone!
              So unwise, he!

" His life a failure! " So I hear you say;
  And who can doubt who looks on earth's suc-
    cess,
Where gilded folly proudly wears the bay
  And simpering millions haste some knave to
    bless?
Fanatic! Yes, according to your rule.
  Foolish! No doubt, in average mankind's
    ken.
A teacher with one lesson for his school;
  Impractical, with faith in love, but then—
              He was The Christ.

'TIS THE SECRET OF YOUTH.

LIFE taught me her lesson; I hold it as truth
That a smile in the heart is the secret of
    youth;
For age cannot harm him, nor do him a wrong,
Who whistles a bit as he journeys along.
The face must be wrinkled, the hair must be
    gray,
But the heart may be young till the end of the
    day,
For ever and ever there standeth the truth:
A smile in the heart is the secret of youth.

What matter the wrinkles, except they shall
    frown?
What matters the silver where once was the
    brown?
For still we may smile though the morning is
    gone,
And the light of that smile is the light of the
    dawn;

And still as we whistle dull care to the wind,
There's a way out of trouble forever we find;
For the ages have told it; they whisper the truth
That a smile in the heart is the secret of youth.

The shoulders must stoop, but the spirit may
      stand
Serene as the dawnlight that kisseth the land.
Old age cannot touch them, the years they defy,
Who smile as life's phantoms go scurrying by.
A sigh is Care's agent to wrinkles enroll,
And a frown is the curtain we drop o'er the soul;
But the spirit still whispers 'mid sorrow and ruth
That a smile in the heart is the secret of youth.

JIM WAS PECULIAR.

JIM was peculiar.   The 'folks all said
   They kind o' suspicioned he's queer in the
     head.
He'd go moonin' along in an absentish way,
An' lots o' the time he had nothin' to say.
An' when he did talk there was no one could
     know
The thing that he'd say, fer his thoughts seemed
     to go
In a style o' their own, an' likely, maybe,
He'd set folks to thinkin', which hurts us, you
     see.

Jim was peculiar.   I rickolleck now
He of'en remarked that he couldn't see how
A hull million dollars could do a man good.
" Do you reckon," he'd say, " he can use it in
     food,
Er drinkin', er housin', er wearin' of clothes?
Well, then, what's the good of it, land only
     knows."
An' then he'd go moonin' and moonin' away,
An', " Jim is peculiar," the neighbors 'ud say.

Jim was peculiar. The children allowed
There wasn't his ekal in all o' the crowd;
An' you'd see 'em a-smilin' when he was around
An' tellin' 'em stories frum flat on the ground,
An' their laughter would sound like notes from
    the choir,
When the angels is singin' an' callin' us higher;
An' the folks, w'en they saw it and heered it,
    would say:
" That Jim gits more queerer an' queerer each
    day."

Jim was peculiar. The day when he lay
At home on his bed while his life ebbed away
He only remarked: " Well, so fer as I know
I've made a few happy; I'm ready to go."
An' the people all come to the funeral then,
An' they mos'ly shed tears at the final amen;
An' they carved on his monument merely this
    word:
" Jim Jones was peculiar, an' so was his Lord."

DEUCE TAKE PHILOSOPHY!

D EUCE take philosophy! I know a way
    Better by far than philosophers know.
Ho, all ye sages with heads turning gray,
    What in the end is the thing you can show?
Is it some knowledge to tell of the how,
    With ne'er a perception of wherefore and why?
What is the morrow? And what is the now?
    And what is the change that we label, to die?

Deuce take philosophy! I know a spot
    Where all of the wisdom of dust-covered tome
And its half-erudition availeth us not—
    'Tis the place where Love reigns in the king-
        dom of Home.
And, oh, ye philosophers, there is a light,
    The light shining forth from the eyes that I
        love,
Which maketh your wisdom to seem as the
        night,
    So high its revealment your knowledge above.

Deuce take philosophy!   Hands that reach out
  To bless me, caress me, and lighten the pain
That comes 'mid the shadows of care and of
      doubt
  To double my labor and deaden my brain,
Yours is the wisdom the sages have missed;
  Yours is the substance, and theirs is the foam.
So I turn from the books to the ones who have
      kissed
  My lips into smiles in the kingdom of Home.

ɩ

OUT IN THE MOUNTAINS.

I WANT to be out in the mountains; I'm tired
of staying here,
With only the everlasting plain outstretching far
or near;
I am weary of the city and the pavement's cease-
less glare,
And I want to be out where God's about and
His glory's everywhere;
I want to lie down on the hillside and dream as
'the white clouds pass,
With no one to tell me I'd better move on, or
warn me, " Keep off the grass;"
I just want a chance to breathe an air that's
never been boxed as yet;
Oh, I'd like to be free as the brown quails be,
with never a care to fret.

I want to be out in the mountains where there's
    room for the soul to grow;
Where the brooks just laugh in their freedom,
    and the hills in the evening glow.
With a rod or a gun as poor excuse, I'd lazily lie
    and dream,
And " Trouble," I'd say, " may go its way; it
    isn't a part of my scheme."
And the trout might leap in the sunlight for all
    of my rod and me,
And the quail might whistle, the deer might run;
    I'd leave them safe and free,
For someway I think in the mountains dear life
    is too sweet to lose;
It is only down here, where we worry and fear,
    that a creature to die might choose.

I want to be out in the mountains where freedom
    is not a name;
Where the soul is glad in its birthright, nor
    walks with the halt and lame;
For peace is upon the summits, and liberty's in
    the vales,
And the heart, oft sad, can only be glad in the
    shadow-haunted dales.
With the birds trilling out in gladness, the flow-
    ers like thoughts of God,
With the blue above and the green beneath, and
    the blossom-sprinkled sod;
With rest, dear rest for the spirit through the
    peaceful, peaceful year,
I want to be out in the mountains; I'm tired of
    staying here.

MY LITTLE MOTHER'S PRAYER.

SHE was just a little woman, not more than
    five feet tall,
But she had a way of working that was bound
    to beat them all.
She would work for me and sister, and her hands
    were never still;
She just kept working, working, as I guess she
    always will.
And all my aunts would say to her: " Now,
    Julia, don't you know
You'll spoil them children sure as fate if you
    keep workin' so
And don't let them do some of it." I s'pose my
    aunts were right,
But still my sister wasn't spoiled, and p'r'aps I
    wasn't—quite.

I never see my mother now, but, wheresoe'er I
    be,
I know that she is working yet and thinking still
    of me;
And sometimes when she's thinking there's a
    film before her eye,
And for me a prayer's ascending to the Father
    up on high.
And, oh, I think I couldn't stray so very far
    from Him,
While that sweet prayer's ascending and those
    dear eyes are dim;
And sometimes as I wander I can almost see her
    there,
With the dear hands working, working, and I
    seem to hear the prayer.

I think the boys whose mothers work, and hope,
    and always pray,
Though they may stumble oftentimes, won't
    wander quite away;
And if they fall, and fall again, they'll rise again,
    for there,
In every lowest depth of sin, they'll hear their
    mother's prayer.

They'll hear it in the stillest night; 'twill follow
    them by day,
And when they falter, " Rise again " 'twill ever,
    ever say.
It reaches down the darkest years; it points to
    guerdons fair.
Few hopeless fall who still recall a mother's lov-
    ing prayer.

Oh, mother, little mother, God's hand has
    touched to gray
The soft brown hair so smooth and fair that I
    recall to-day,
Though the faithful hands still labor for the ones
    they love the best,
As they will toil unto the end, until He giveth·
    rest;
Yet I think sometimes that they must fold,
    while comes the misty host
Of visions of the girl and boy for whom they
    toiled the most;
And I long that you shall feel and know, as you
    sit dreaming there,
That your boy in love remembers every faithful
    deed and prayer.

AS THE YEARS GO BY.

FOREVER and ever the suns go down;
  Forever and ever they rise again;
And life is a maid with a golden crown
  And sandals of darkness beloved by men.
We are dreaming to-day of a future of bliss;
  To-morrow we bury the hope with a sigh,
With a long, long sigh and a farewell kiss—
  And that is the way that the years go by.

" To-morrow," we say, " I will build me a home
  In the beautiful, beautiful land of rest."
But the morrow comes and our feet yet roam,
  And our hearts are sad and our lives unblest,
And the suns smile down on our falling tears,
  And the friends we love are the ones who die,
And the phantom of pleasure is chased by fears—
  And that is the way that the years go by.

Forever and ever we say at night:
  " Oh, woeful to-morrow, to bring me pain! "
But the morrow comes, and the sun is bright,
    And the loss that we dreaded has turned to
      gain;
And the flowers of joy in our souls still bloom,
    And the smile of the spirit has followed its
      sigh,
And the daybeams of gladness have banished the
      gloom—
    And that is the way that the years go by.

Forever and ever—oh, valley of life,
  Where joy is a phantom and woe is a shade !
Mocked by our visions no less than our strife,
  What is the game when the game is played ?
Who is the Player whose pawns are we,
  Who sits in the mists as the moments fly?
Who is the One that the end doth see,
  As the phantoms fade and the years go by ?

MY DAUGHTER'S PRISCILLA.

M Y daughter's Priscilla. I know not how
　　She came to my life from the Puritan
　　　　days,
With the calm, true eyes and the tranquil brow
　　And the voice as sweet as a hymn of praise;
But if some picture from days of old
　　Might step from its place in an oaken frame,
Bearing no trace of the gray past's mold,
　　I fancy that picture would look the same—

The same as my daughter, whose calm, slow eyes
　　Look to my own, while the love shines
　　　　through,
As a star ray pierces the evening skies
　　Or a sunbeam cleaves through the dome of
　　　　blue.
In the touch of her hand all comfort dwells,
　　And Peace through her dear lips makes her
　　　　plea,
For her voice is sweet as a chime of bells—
　　My daughter Priscilla, who blesses me.

My daughter's Priscilla. Ah me ! Ah me !
  My heart is turbulent, wild and worn;
But her tranquil eyes I need but see,
  And the cloak of unrest from my soul is torn.
I know not how—I say it again—
  She came from the past with her eyes a-shine,
But this I cry to my soul's amen :
  " I thank the Father that she is mine."

AT THE BOTTOM OF THE SEA.

D O you think you'd like to be at the bottom
        of the sea,
    With the pollyhinkus swinging all around,
And the gogglers with their eyes big as mama's
        custard pies,
    And the winkus that goes crawling on the
        ground,
                And the spry,
                (Oh, my eye !)
                The spry, spry, spry,
The very, very, very, very spry springaree
    That slides through the glare of the water
        everywhere,
On the shifting, lifting bottom of the deep blue
        sea ?

At the bottom of the sea there is strangest mys-
    tery,
  For the queen of all the sprites is living there,
With amber beads for eyes, and she lives on oys-
    ter fries,
  And she hates to hear the wicked sailors swear;
        And her hair,
        It is fair;
        It is fair, fair, fair;
It is very, very, very, very, very bright and fair;
  And the fishes swim about through her palace
    in and out,
Through the water that is shifting and is lifting
    everywhere.

But I want to tell you, dear, and I hope that you
    will hear,
  That really it is better to be living on the
    ground,
Where the things are not so queer, but the at-
    mosphere is clear,
  And in order to enjoy it 'tisn't needful to be
    drowned;
            For you know
            (It is so,
            And you should know, know)
It is really, really chilly where the dim depths be;
  And it's surely very tough; yes, it certainly is
    rough,
For you can't breathe a little in the deep blue
    sea.

LITTLE WHITE SISTER.

OH, little white Sister, secluded out yonder,
　　Saying your Aves from day unto day,
What are your hopes and your visions, I wonder.
　What are your fancies of life and its way ?
Know you the burdens, the cares and the losses
　Waiting the weary outside of your door ?
Know you how heavy, how heavy the crosses ?
　Know you the hearts that are troubled and
　　　sore ?
　　　　Little white Sister,
　　　　　Tell me, I pray,
　　　　What do you dream
　　　　　As the years grow gray ?

Oh, little white Sister, your heart has its fan-
    cies—
  I look in your eyes and I know it is so—
They steal from your soul in the half-timid
    glances,
  Then steal again back, as a spirit might go.
Your voice is so quiet, I wonder, I wonder
  If the charm of contentment you really have
    found.
Does peace indeed dwell your white raiment un-
    der ?
  Does your spirit's horizon no mist of doubt
    bound ?
      Little white Sister,
        Tell me, I pray,
      Does peace in your breast
        Dwell ever and aye ?

Oh, little white Sister, out here in the battle
  The smoke of the struggle envelops us all;
We lose His low voice in the musketry's rattle,
  And the mad dream of glory still holds us in
      thrall;
And we drag on our chains, or iron or golden,
  And we cry at the last that this life is a lie;
And we turn dreamy eyes to the days that are
    olden—
  Do the years with you, Sister, glide peacefully
    by ?
        Little white Sister,
         Tell me, I pray,
        Is your soul at peace,
         Removed from the fray ?

Oh, little white Sister, in gentle petitions
  I pray you remember one soul of unrest;
Shorn of his happiness, mocked by ambitions,
    Cross little white hands for him over your
      breast;
For he has forgotten—the battle's so dreary!—
    The words that he learned at a dear mother's
      knee,
And his heart it is dumb—for life is a-weary!
    Little white Sister, reach upward, for me.
        Little white Sister,
          Peace unto thee;
        In gentle petitions
          Remember thou me.

THE SCHOOLGIRL THAT I HATED.

SOMETIMES when memory draws the veil
    and I look back a way
To where the sun was shining in my happy,
    youthful day
I catch the scent of lilacs as they blossomed by
    our door,
And I hear the robins chirping as they used to
    chirp of yore,
And the oriole is flitting like a ball of living fire,
And the river's sort o' whispering just as though
    'twould never tire;
And then, amid the faces that on memory's
    screen I see,
Comes the schoolgirl that I hated when she sat
    in front of me.

Someway I see her plainly now in scanty dress of
    blue,
With eyes in part coquettish and in part serene
    and true;
With curls that liked to catch the light and twist
    it in and out,
And lips just right for kissing, if they *were* in-
    clined to pout.
I knew that she was pretty, but I said she was no
    good—
Though I couldn't help admiring her; no boy
    that's human could—
But she made up faces at me, and she could a
    vixen be,
The schoolgirl that I hated when she sat in front
    of me.

She wouldn't play at marbles, and she couldn't
 play at ball,
And I often intimated that she was no good at
 all.
I dropped a cricket down her back in cheerful,
 boyish way,
And she yelled first; then I yelled next, when
 teacher was to pay.
She wouldn't " coon " a melon, though I asked
 her oftentimes,
And she ridiculed my first attempts at poor and
 broken rhymes.
Oh, she was a thorough failure, as any boy can
 see,
The schoolgirl that I hated when she sat in front
 of me.

She beat me at the lessons that we found within
    our books,
And when she went above me all scornful were
    her looks;
But when the teacher whipped me I saw her cry
    one day,
And I said that " girls is better than what some
    fellers say; "
And I sort of half forgave her for her lack of
    hardihood,
Though I even then insisted that she really was
    no good;
But times have changed since then, for I—I'm
    married, don't you see,
To the schoolgirl that I hated when she sat in
    front of me.

IF DREAMS WERE GOLD.

IF dreams were gold I'd build for you,
　My love, my own, a palace fair
As Babylonian monarchs knew,
　And you should dwell right regnant there.
For, oh, my love, I've wealth of dreams;
　They press upon my waking brain.
Half glad, half sad that pressure seems,
　Like the strange joy akin to pain.

If dreams were gold, dear heart, dear heart,
　The realm of beauty were your own,
And skilled designers of the mart
　Should weave and build for you alone.
For, oh, these dreams whose glories shine
　Within my heart, within my soul,
Their joy, alas, is only mine;
　And I would give to you the whole.

If dreams were gold—Oh, love of mine,
  Full well I know, who sit and dream,
That gold ne'er bought one bliss divine;
  No heaven answers to its gleam.
Then since I dream—I know not why—
  And since the dreams are mine alone,
Let all the lack of part supply,
  And take the dreamer for your own.

Take the poor dreamer, and his dreams
  Shall bathe you in their mellow light,
As in some vale the moonlight gleams
  About the rose asleep at night;
And we shall richer be, I trow,
  Ay, richer by a wealth untold,
Than any riches we might know
  If dreams were gold, if dreams were gold.

WHEN THE STARS SLEEP.

W HEN the little stars sleep, they rest, we
know,
On the cloudland's misty pillows,
Till the sun creeps over the western world
And is drowned in the ocean billows;
Then straightway they peep from their chamber
out,
A watch on the gray earth keeping,
But the world rolls on, with its toil and doubt,
And it cares not a whit for their peeping.

The world rolls on, and its children sing
A song to the rhythm of pleasure,
Till the Player strikes a minor string
And slower, and slow, is the measure.
Passion and Happiness, Joy and Shame,
Join hands while the world is dreaming—
Still the stars look down from their heights of
flame,
God's peace o'er the tumult beaming.

Then the sun comes up o'er the eastern land,
  And the stars creep back in wonder,
Till he tucks them away with his great white
    hand,
  The sky's blue coverlet under;
But all of the day they wait and wait,
  And all of its moments they measure,
Till they look again on that strange, mad dance—
  The dance to the rhythm of pleasure.

IN THE CITY, THE CITY.

IN the city, the city, the fog creeps in
To hide with its curtain the phantom of sin,
And the fever of hurry has seized on all,
The rich and the poor, and it holds them in
    thrall;
And they race with Time till the race is run,
And the grave is the goal that the effort won,
And they push and jostle and scheme and plot
In the city, the city, where God is not.

In the city, the city, I note the care
That gnaws at a life till the life is bare;
And the children who skulk in the alleys, all
Are old from their birth and pinched and small.
There are women who live in a self-made hell,
And their hearts beat on like a funeral knell;
And lives like the nightshade blossom and rot
In the city, the city, where God is not.

In the city, the city, I long to rest
Where the hills stoop down to the crimson west,
Where the brooks leap down from the summer's
      snow
And the poppied fields are with flame aglow,
Where the squirrels hide and the brown quail
      nest
And God sets a seal on the soul's unrest.
To the hills and the mountains, each peace-
      breeding spot,
I turn from the city, where God is not.

CITY AND COUNTRY WAYS.

I GUESS that I can never git much used to
city ways.
Someway in dodging through the streets I feel
I'm in a maze,
And when some driver runs me down, or almost
does, before
I know he's anywhere around, I jump a rod or
more
An' give a yell, the while he laughs and says,
" You fool, git out! "
I wish that I was back again and jus' a loafin'
'bout
An' knowin' all my neighbors' biz an' tendin' to
it, too,
The way that country people can an' almost
always do.

When these here waggins that they run without
    no horses on
Comes slidin' up to where I am an' scare me till
    I'm wan,
I always wish that I could be back where the
    country lies
Jus' sort o' reachin' out to God and smilin' to
    His skies.
I want to go back there again an' hear the peo-
    ple say:
" Waal, how's your inflooenzy now, and how's
    the kid to-day? "
Fer city folks don't know my biz an' sort o' run
    it, too,
The way that country people can an' almost
    always do.

Of course I know the city folks has theatres an'
    all,
But when the baby's middlin' sick they hardly
    ever call;
They don't drop in an' say, " B'gee! D'you hear
    that Bilkins' twins
Has took the measles?—Punishment, I s'pose,
    fer father's sins."
An' when my rheumatiz comes on an' breaks my
    needed rest
There's not a wave of trouble rolls across their
    peaceful breast.
An' so I say I want to go where folks my biz'll
    run,
The way the country folks I know have almost
    always done.

THE OLDEN DAYS, THE GOLDEN DAYS.

THE olden days, the golden days, the days
    when we were young,
When life was all a hymn of praise and we the
    ones who sung;
The laughter of that elder time comes ringing
    back to me,
The echo of a silvery chime from o'er a widening
    sea;
And still I hear both sweet and clear the voices
    hushed and low,
Like whispers from another sphere, of friends of
    long ago.
Like some gray ghost my spirit strays the
    ghosts of dawn among
And sighs to praise the olden days, the days
    when we were young.

The olden days, the golden days—oh, boyhood's
heart of fire,
Is this the ending of the ways?   For this didst
thou aspire?
A dream that ended in a dream?   A hope now
lying dead?
A little time to toil and scheme with naught but
gloom o'erhead?
Is this the answer life must give unto its promise
fair?
Hopes, idle hopes, that may not live, and faith
that fights despair?
A dream that never pain allays?   A halting, lisping tongue?
Oh, better far the olden days, the days when we
were young.

The olden days, the golden days when care was
    all unknown,
Still back to them my memory strays and there
    it dwells alone,
Alone and lonely, yet 'tis blessed, for so they
    cheer me yet,
The ones who wandered or do rest unheeding
    care and fret.
Far fields of clover all abloom, low hills my boy-
    hood knew,
From the dim present and its gloom, I turn, I
    turn to you;
From the drear maze of weary days with clouds
    of doubt o'erhung,
I turn to days, the golden days, the days when
    we were young.

TO THE PIONEERS THAT REMAIN.

I HAVE no word to speak their praise.
Theirs was the deed; the guerdon ours.
The wilderness and weary days
Were theirs alone; for us the flowers.
They sowed the seed that we might reap;
Ours is the fruitage of their years.
And now, behold, they drop to sleep,
And we have naught for them save tears.

The flag, whose luster none may mar,
The brightest thing that loves the air,
See you our California's star
Amidst the rest? They set it there.
What wonder that it droops to-day,
The while another folds his hands,
And, silent, floats away, away,
From golden sands to golden sands.

So they go out.   A little while,
   And none shall answer to the call.
Still shall the great world weep or smile,
   But they shall be all silent—all.
Still shall the life-tides ebb and flow
   And mark the rhythm of the years,
But they no more shall heed or know,
   Forgotten cares and hopes and fears.

When they are gone; when o'er one's clay
   Our tears of long farewell shall fall,
We'll pay our tribute then, and say:
   " He was the last, the last of all.
Ah, they were stalwart men," we'll sigh,
   " The future's promise on each brow."
So shall we whisper then, but I—
   I pay that tribute here and now.

A LITTLE, LITTLE FELLOW.

THERE'S a little, little fellow, and he's really
    very small,
For he measures by my table and he isn't quite
    so tall;
And this little, little fellow in the evening seeks
    my knees,
And he says: "Now won't oo tell me jus' the
    nicest 'tories, p'ease?"
And then I tell him stories that I wouldn't dare
    to say
Are of the usual run of things we meet on every
    day;
And the last thing that he asks me is, with story-
    telling through,
"Now do you 'pose when I'm growed up I'll
    know as much as you?"

Oh, little, little fellow, who sit upon my knee,
I know how all misplaced is this, the faith you
    rest in me.
My wisdom is a fiction, and my stock of knowl-
    edge small;
Like you, I guess the Father knows, and He is
    over all.
I stumble on the journey and I falter as I go,
And where the days shall lead me I never, never
    know.
But, though I'm all unworthy of your faith, it
    cheers me, too,
With " Do you 'pose when I'm growed up I'll
    know as much as you? "

Oh, little, little fellow, I really hope you will.
I want to feel when I leave off you'll be advanc-
ing still;
And if sometimes I half have seen a light beyond
the mist,
I trust that by its purest rays your pathway may
be kissed.
But whatsoe'er the years may bring, and whatsoe'er their lore,
Someway I'm hoping here to-night, as I have
hoped before,
That you may keep some part, at least, of faith
in me you knew
When oft you asked if " when I'm growed I'll
know as much as you."

WHO KNEW THIS MAN ?

GOD touched his eyes, and then, no doubt,
      he saw
  What other men may only vaguely guess;
Behind dumb sorrow saw the loving Law,
    And knew His wisdom sendeth pain to bless.
He saw (though dimly) that behind the deed
    There stands the Doer waiting the event;
So o'er the rocks where human feet must bleed
    He walked, though bruised, with calm and full
        content—
          God touched his eyes.

God touched his heart, and, lo, he felt the pain
    Of those dread sorrows borne by human kind;
To help another counted surest gain,
    And lost himself that he might others find.
Oh, ne'er a hand outreached to him in vain,
    For " I must love them " was his tender
        thought;
He wiped the eyes bewet with trouble's rain,
    Till glorious manhood for himself he
        wrought—
          God touched his heart.

God touched his soul.   The clink of yellow gold
   He counted nothing save to better men;
For selfish ends the stuff he could not hold,
   But saw dread want and let it go again.
Alone he walked, yet blessed by all he knew;
   Alone he lived, but hundreds loved his name;
Into the lives of careworn men he grew,
   And saw and felt dull sorrow's strenuous
      claim—
      God touched his soul.

God touched his life.   One night they found him
      there,
   With smile of welcome for the angel gray;
But Death himself could only make him fair,
   And peace was with him, as he, dreaming, lay.
And then they came, glad youth and somber age,
   And stood beside that humble, lowly bed,
And tears fell fast that nothing might assuage,
   And, " Much I loved him;" it was all they
      said—
      God touched his life.

THE BOYS OF THE COUNTRY PRESS.

THE boys, the boys of the country press
   Who strive and toil while their "pile"
     grows less,
Who take in potatoes and wood and hay
And corn and mutton and beans for pay,
Who write heavy leaders, and set them, too;
Who say, "Well, I guess that these beans will
     do
When the flour gives out," nor whistle the less—
I sing to the boys of the country press.

I sing to the boys—God bless them all!
Who sit in their sanctums drear and small,
While the partisan tells them why times are bad,
And the merchant drops in to stop his "ad,"
And the parson explains theological things,
And the granger remarks, as his trophy he
     brings:
"Naow this here pertater's the socker, I
     guess"—
I sing to the boys of the country press.

I sing to the boys in a humble place
Who turn to the days a resolute face,
Who feel that each duty has something to bless,
Though they bow to the sweep of the old hand-
     press;
The boys who toil on till their toiling is done,
As editor, foreman and typo in one,
With people who curse them, and others to
     bless—
I sing to the boys of the country press.

I sing to the boys—may a blessing fall
On the toilers who sit in the sanctums small!
And if patient endeavor is worthy its prize,
If the low path of duty leads on to the skies,
If there's never an effort, how lowly soe'er,
But its certain fruition draws steadily near,
Why, then, when the shadows have folded, I
     guess
The One who is leading and guiding to bless
His subscription will pay to the country press.

WE SHALL REST SWEETLY.

WE shall lie down to the infinite rest,
    E'en as the millions before us.
Sweetly we'll sleep on the great Mother's breast,
    The calm, tender Mother that bore us.
Passion of loving and tumult of strife,
    They shall be buried forever;
With white hands enfolded we'll look back to life
    And smile at its weary endeavor.

We shall rest sweetly—oh, wonderful rest!—
As a babe lies asleep on its dear mother's breast;
Trials forgotten and errors confessed,
    We shall rest sweetly, so sweetly.

Haply through eyelids down drooping shall steal
  A vision One sendeth to cheer us,
White homes of peace that the earth-mists con-
    ceal,
  Loved ones and vanished ones near us.
Haply from out of the little, low room
  A stairway and star-way shall lead us
To the country of light from the valley of gloom,
  Where angels shall guide us and heed us.

We shall rest sweetly down under the sod,
Knowing the stairway that leads up to God,
The crystal white star-way by angel-feet trod—
  We shall rest sweetly, so sweetly.

I JUDGED HE WAS RIGHT.

E F the crops was good Brother Ephrum
         would say,
" Well, I jedge that the price'll be low, anyway;"
An' if prices was good he'd say, " Well, I fear
They're goin' to be down in the suller nex'
         year;"
Ef ever'thing went jest es smooth es could be,
He'd look to the futur', an' trouble he'd see,
An' he'd say: " Well, per'aps it's all right, but,
         I jing!
I'm mightily skeered what nex' season'll bring."
         That's the way that he talked.

Ef the weather was windy he said that he knowed
The buds frum the dern apple trees would be
         blowed;
Ef a fortnight went by with no signs of a rain
He said that a drowth was a-comin' again;

An' he said that the wheat would be half of a
    crop,
Fer the bugs was jus' certain to eat it all up;
An' his fav'rite expression was allers: " I jing!
I'm mightily skeered what nex' season'll bring."
        It was allers that way.

One day Brother Ephrum was passin' away,
An' the fambily gathered to hear what he'd say.
But he didn't say much, jest heavin' some sighs,
W'ile the mists was a-gatherin' in front of his
    eyes,
But at last a low whisper the fambily heard,
An' o' course they stooped down so's to catch
    every word;
But all that he uttered was only: " I jing!
I'm mightily skeered what nex' season'll bring."
        An' I jedged he was right.

A SONG FOR THE LITTLE CHAPS.

HERE is a song for the little chaps,
　　The little, wee fellows who don't know
　　　why
The round world turns; and I guess, perhaps,
　　That neither do you and neither do I.
Here is a song for the comical mites,
　　Round and rosy and fat and sleek,
Who gaze in amaze on the world's queer sights;
　　And here is the blessing I cannot speak.

Here is a song for the ones that gaze
　　In queer consternation on finger and toe,
And note they are moving in speechless amaze,
　　And wonder who wound them and made the
　　　things go.
The dear little fellows who deem mother's breast
　　Is all of the world, and a good world, too,
I am singing to them, while they lie at rest;
　　And really what better is there to do?

Here is a song for the babes that stand
　Nearer to God than the grown folk do;
Fresh little buds from the Heaven-land
　Who deem that the world is fresh and new.
Bundles of helplessness, dearer than all
　Yet born of the morning and kissed by its
　　dew;
Feeble and wondering, blinking and small,
　Babes whom I love, I am singing to you.

WE WEARY OF IT ALL.

WHO does not weary of it all,
    Of hope so high, fulfillment bare;
  The petty strife, the petty care,
And doubt which holds the soul in thrall?

Of little jealousies we feed,
  Of that incessant, spiteful cry,
  " I fear that he is more than I,"
When both of us are small indeed?

Our hands fall down like leaden things,
  But soon we lift them with a frown
  And strive to tear our brother down
From that low height whereto he clings.

And " This," we say, " this ceaseless strife,
  Which bids us when one falls rejoice,"—
  But, oh, the wailing in the voice!—
" This constant warfare, this is life."

And so we build for some poor prize
  Our foolish structure on the sand
  Until it crumbles 'neath our hand,
And, " God," we cry, " our dreams are lies."

And if one holds a clearer thought,
  A faith, a hope no red earth bribes,
  " Oho," we cry, with mocking gibes,
" He is a dreamer and distraught.

" He is a savior. Crucify ! "—
  Oh, mad, mad world, thy Calvary
  Still bears its bitter fruit for thee,
And still to love is but to die.

Oh, God, we weary of it all,
  Of this incessant, cruel strife;
  Of grief, of hatred, aye, of life;
We weary, and we wait Thy call.

A LULLABY.

SLEEP, my little one, where you float
On the Dreamland Sea in the Dreamland
     Boat;
But where is that sea and whither you go,
Ah, who is so wise that he ever may know?
There the sails of the voyager onward are fanned
By the lullaby breezes from Hushabyland,
And the boat is a cradle that swings to and fro,
But whither it bears you, ah, none of us know.

   Sleep, my little one.   None may know
     Whither the Dreamboat saileth,
   But One heedeth ever wherever you go,
     And His is a love never faileth.

Sleep, my little one, sleep and dream
As you float, float away on the wonderful stream
That leads to the land where the white angels be,
Which I, in my blindness, no longer may see.
There the Angel of Love and the Angel of Rest
Shall cuddle my bairnie so close to the breast
That only the thought of the mother and me
Could bring you safe home again over the sea.

Sleep, my little one, sleep and smile,
  Floating, ah, none may know whither;
You shall sail back again after a while,
  Guided by angel hands hither.

IT IS WELL TO REMEMBER.

IT is well to remember this thing, you know:
　Though the rains may descend and the winds
　　may blow;
Though the skies may be dark as the hour of
　fate,
And our latter be worse than our former state,
Yet over the clouds there is always the sun,
And the stars will appear when the tempest is
　done;
　　And the soul needs its woe—
　　'Neath the rain, flowers grow—
It is well to remember this thing, you know.

It is well to remember this thing, you know:
The stalwart may stand 'neath the cruelest blow.
For the soul, tempest driven, must turn to its
　God,
As the rain-beaten flowers look up from the sod;
And the fragrance of love is the price of our
　pain,
As the blossoms grow sweet 'neath the blows of
　the rain.
　　Heigh-ho and heigh-ho !
　　We weep, but we grow,
And it's well to remember this thing, you know.

WAITING FOR SANTA CLAUS.

THEY say he's but a pretty myth, the Santa
    Claus I knew
When I was but a little chap, with little notions,
    too;
They say he doesn't go about with reindeers and
    a sleigh,
And lots and lots of toys and things he means to
    give away.
But let them say whate'er they please, I not the
    less must feel
That few indeed are things of life so very, very
    real
As was the joy of girl and boy—say not it lacked
    a cause—
When mother tucked us in our bed to wait for
    Santa Claus.

"Now go to sleep," our mother said—ah, still
 the words I hear,—
But how on earth could children sleep when
 Santa Claus was near?
And so we whispered for a time and rolled and
 tumbled some,
And felt assured that Christmas morn would
 never, never come,
Until at length the elves of sleep tied down our
 lashes fast,
And gently we sailed o'er the sea—the dream-
 land sea—at last;
And in the morning ere the sun first peeped our
 windows through—
Don't tell me Santa didn't come; I guess we
 children knew.

Don't tell me Santa didn't come—O, dreamland
    girl and boy,
It was no fiction that you knew a joy surpassing
    joy.
White-robed, I hear you patter still across the
    bedroom floor
To delve within the stockings' depths for toys,
    and yet for more.
If this be fiction I recall, then by my sager years
I vow that they are phantoms all—our hopes,
    and e'en our fears.
And I am wishing here to-night, despite cold
    wisdom's laws,
That mother now might tuck us in to wait for
    Santa Claus.

AS I WOULD BELIEVE.

I WANT to keep thinking that God's as true,
And the grass as green and the skies as blue,
As they used to be when my life was young
And the bird of the morn to my spirit sung.
I want to look out through my time-dimmed
      eyes
To the ships of mist in the sea of skies,
And feel that the hand that guides them there
Will still for my faltering footsteps care.

For someway I think as the years grow old
And our heads turn gray that our hearts grow
      cold;
And I'd like to keep the old-time trust,
Lest my soul shall turn to ashes and dust;
I would like to hold my faith in man,
Nor his life's emotion with coldness scan;
I fain would *believe*, as I used to do,
When my life was young and its skies were blue.

For I'd sooner have faith in one heart's truth,
As I did in the days of my golden youth,
Than, knowing the world, lose faith and sigh:
" Ah,. hope's a delusion and life is a lie! "
I would sooner believe, though it prove me a
     fool,
That the Teacher is heeding our lessons in
     school
Than moan to the night: " It all is vain,
And the object of pain is only—pain."

So I'll cling to the trust that I'm battling here—
Though it be with a sigh or a falling tear— _
For an end that is hidden the mist behind;
And I'll dream that His purpose is always kind.
Let it prove me a fool, if you will.   I say
That I'd sooner press on in such simple way
Than, knowing o'er much (which Is nothing),
     sigh:
" Alas!   I have lived, but my life was a lie."

AS I LIE HERE AND DREAM.

A S I lie here and dream I hear
A mead'lark whistling sweet and clear,
And straightly then his mate replies
From yonder where the willow lies.
" Oh, life is sweet," he sings alway;
" And love is life," she hastes to say.
And then they sing together so
That angels listen where they go—
   As I lie here and dream.

As I lie here the river flows,
And whispers to me as it goes,
And just one word it seems to say,
Just "Peace" and "Peace" and "Peace" alway.
And soon the world grows hushed and still;
Down drops the sun behind its hill,
And, " Soul, be silent," low I say,
" For now is Nature going to pray "—
   As I lie here and dream.

As I lie here the stars creep out
And wink their eyes and look about.
A katydid chirps out its cheer,
And then there sound, or far or near,
The tiny voices of the night,
And all the world is hushed and white;
And straight are banished care and doubt—
They are so small when God's about—
      As I lie here and dream.

A SONG FOR THE UNDER DOG.

NOW here is a song for the under dog, the
    weak under dog in the fight,
For though he is down, and he's terribly down,
    mayhap he's the dog that is right.
It isn't the cur who is largest, you know, whose
    morals are always the best,
And a sanctified pup with a halo, I trow, might
    succumb in a physical test.
If might could make right—but it cannot, you
    see, and I think you'll admit it were quaint
If a blacksmith must always the best of men be,
    and a bruiser must pose as a saint.
The man who succeeds may succeed as a knave,
    and in morals fly fearfully light,
And that's why your sympathy kindly I crave for
    the weak under dog in the fight.

The martyrs who died for the cause that they
    deemed was surely the cause of their God,
From whose wounds, gaping widely, the life-
    blood has streamed till it reddened the
    blossoming sod;
The martyrs who gave—it was all they could
    do—their lives for the truth and the right,
What were they, bethink you with sorrow and
    rue, but man's under dogs in the fight?
Perhaps in the far-away end—but who knows?
    and your guess is no better than mine,
For we preface our knowledge always with
    " suppose " as the great verb " to live " we
    decline.
So, putting all guesses straightway to the rear, it
    seemeth most certainly right
To take off our hats and to heartily cheer for the
    weak under dog in the fight.

So here is my cheer for the poor under dog. He
    is not the strongest, but then,
It may hap that he's better by far than the dog
    that chews him again and again.
His stock may be finer, his loyalty proved, and I
    think you will hardly demur
When I say that quite often the dog on the top
    is the scurviest kind of a cur.
And as the rule runs in the big canine world, so
    it runs with us humans, I know;
Too often some cur of a man is on top, with a
    really good fellow below,
And that's why I'm singing as best I know how
    this lame little anthem to-night
To the poor, hungry devil who's clear out of
    luck—the weak under dog in the fight.

WHAT IS THE DREAM IN MY BABY'S EYES?

WHAT is the dream in the baby's eyes,
As she lies and blinks in mute surprise?
With little, wee hands that aimlessly go
Hither and thither and to and fro;
With little, wee feet that shall lead her—God
knows,
But a prayer from my heart like a benison goes;
Bundle of helplessness, yonder she lies—
What is the dream in my baby's eyes ?

What does she wonder, and what does she know
That we have forgotten so long, long ago?
Bathed in the dawnlight, what does she see
That slow years have hidden from you and from
me?
Out of the yesterdays, seeth she yet
The things that in living she soon shall forget,
All that is hidden beyond the blue skies?
What is the dream in my baby's eyes?

Speak to me, little one, ere you forget:
What is the thought that is lingering yet?
Where is the land where the yesterdays meet,
Waiting and waiting the morrows to greet?
You wee, funny bundle, who only will blink,
What do you wonder, and what do you think?
Blue as the moonlight asleep in the skies,
What is the dream in my baby's eyes?

MY GRANDSIRE'S " LET US PRAY."

WHEN the morning meal was ended, my
grandsire used to say:
" Let us ask our Heavenly Father now to help
us through the day."
Then he took the well-worn Bible from the little
corner stand,
And read about the glories of the happy, prom-
ised land.
There was just a little quaver in his voice when-
e'er he read
How the One who loved the people had not
where to lay His head,
But he told in tone triumphant how the stead-
fast win the fray;
Then closed the book with reverence, softly saying: " Let us pray."

Our Heavenly Father, in Thy hands
Our lives are placed for keeping.
Guard us in mercy through the day;
Watch over us while sleeping;
And, if we sin, in love forgive;
Thou knowest all our blindness.
In darkness groping, still we trust
Ourselves unto Thy kindness.

It was a little homely prayer, old fashioned if
  you will,
But in my heart it's echoing yet and never will
  be still.
Its only eloquence or charm was on my grand-
  sire's face,
Yet I'm certain that it mounted to the Father's
  throne of grace;
And I think the angels listened just to hear the
  reverent tone
In which that gray-haired Christian made his
  wants and sorrows known;
And though my feet have wandered oft from
  duty's narrow way
Somehow I feel I'm better for my grandsire's
  " Let us pray."

  Oh, teach us, Father, that Thy way
    Is always one of beauty,
  And guide us lest our feet shall stray
    From out the path of duty.
  Life's hill is rugged, Father; lead, ·
    Oh, lead us safely on;
  Fit thou Thy mercy to our need,
    Till robes of light we don.

The prayer was long. I still recall how I would
    squirm and wriggle,
And at my sister faces make till she perforce
    must giggle;
Yet, through the recklessness of youth, some
    words of human pleading
Would touch the boy and make him think of
    paths to Heaven leading.
The kindness on that dear old face was written
    like a blessing;
The love and peace that lingered there are past
    my poor expressing,
But I know that I am better for the words he
    used to say
When he closed the Bible gently, saying softly,
    " Let us pray."

    Oh, Thou, who blessed the children here
      And held them in Thy keeping,
    Bless Thou these two to us so dear,
      Thy mercies on them heaping.
    Through weary ways their feet must go;
      Temptation will assail them,
    But Thou wilt loving kindness show
      And never, never fail them.

'Tis many years since he went home, by God's
 own angels greeted—
I know in Heaven's foremost row the rare old
 man is seated.
No more I hear his loving words, no more his
 kindly greeting,
But if I live one-half as well there'll be another
 meeting.
My feet have wandered oftentimes; I caused him
 care and worry;
I'd like to take his hand in mine and tell him " I
 am sorry; "
And there's one thing I hope he knows up in the
 land of day:
I've always been the better for his gentle " Let
 us pray."

WHEN WHEAT IS WORTH A DOLLAR.

W HEN wheat is worth a dollar, with a tendency to rise,
On the horny-handed granger there are scarcely
any flies;
And he often stops to chuckle 'mid the labors of
the day,
And to ask the passing stranger, " Have you
read the markets? Hay! "
And his smile's a combination of a chasm and a
hole
And there's not a wave of trouble stirs his opti-
mistic soul,
As he says: " They call us hayseeds, but I
reckon we're no guys,
When wheat is worth a dollar, with a tendency
to rise."

When wheat is worth a dollar—I wish that I
    could stand
Among the honest grangers, with a pitchfork in
    my hand;
With a pitchfork for an emblem, and a granary
    full of wheat,
And a cinch upon that mortgage that would
    seem amazing sweet.
I would not be a banker, nor with the bankers
    stand,
But I yearn to be a granger of the horny-handed
    brand;
Then my hayseed jubilate would uplift the
    vaulted skies—
When wheat is worth a dollar, with a tendency
    to rise.

When wheat is worth a dollar and still is going
    up;
When the farmer drinks the nectar Nature pours
    into his cup;
When his smile is broad and beaming, and his
    laugh is like a roar
As he sees the golden gleaming of the wheat he
    has in store,
Then I hope congratulations are a thing that's
    rather neat,
From a man who isn't farming and is mighty
    short of wheat,
For be sure that I extend them, as this pean will
    advise,
When wheat is worth a dollar, with a tendency
    to rise.

THE LAND WHERE OUR DREAMS COME TRUE.

IN the land where our dreams come true, little
      one,
  In the land where our dreams come true,
We will bathe in the waters of Aidenn that run
From the glorified land, from the land of the sun,
And we'll joy in the prize that our life-effort won,
  In the land where our dreams come true,
      Little one,
  In the land where our dreams come true.

There are those whom we loved in the long, long
      ago,
  In the land where our dreams come true,
And we'll look in their eyes with the lovelight
      aglow,
And we'll walk by their side where the calm
      waters flow,
With a peace in our hearts that the glorified
      know,
  In the land where our dreams come true,
      Heigh-ho,
  In the land where our dreams come true.

The hopes that have perished shall waken again,
    In the land where our dreams come true;
They will troop to our side from the yesterdays'
      fen,
From the valley of doubting, the shadowy glen;
They will come with a blessing to children of
      men,
    In the land where our dreams come true,
        Do you ken,
    In the land where our dreams come true.

So we'll turn from the past and its wrack, dear
      heart,
    To the land where our dreams come true;
Where the miles shall not sunder or hold us
      apart,
But the hope that we knew into being shall start,
And to know and to love is the ultimate art,
    In the land where our dreams come true,
        Dear heart,
    In the land where our dreams come true.

(

HERE'S TO THE MAN WHO RISES AGAIN.

N OW here's to the man who rises again!
 I know that the battle is long;
We dream of the morrows, and dreaming is vain,
 Downbeat in the maddening throng.
We walk and we stumble; we fall as we go,
 'And our hopes are but written in vain,
But we still may arise from the heaviest blow,
Stand stalwart, erect, with our face to the foe;
And there's no one more worthy of honor, I
  trow,
 Than the man who arises again.

We are down in the valley; the mists are about,
 The pitfalls lie close at our feet;
We send our Ideals to turmoil and rout,
 And many's the failure we meet;

We are crushed in the struggle; we're weary and
    worn,
    And we feel that our hopes are in vain.
But still in the battle we're held and upborne
By the thought that not vainly we sigh and we
    mourn;
Though the burden of failure in anguish we've
    worn,
    We may rise to our stature again.

To throw and to lose is a wearisome tale,
    A tale that is old as the sun;
But who dares to write that the thrower shall fail
    Till the sum of his throwing is done?
In the uttermost failure success may be writ,
    For we stumble, the height to attain;
In the wardrobe of nature there's not a misfit,
And the height over yonder is ours, I submit,
If, crushed and downfallen, we still strive for it,
    And rise, though we're stricken, again.

HER FAITH NEVER FALTERS.

MY little daughter comes to me,
  And whispers, " I am sorry; "
And I—I take her on my knee
  And tell her not to worry;
And then I kiss her, and she knows
  How tenderly I love her.
We're just two children, I suppose;
  I not a whit above her.

And then she lays her cheek to mine,
  And says, " I love you dearly; "
And in my eyes the teardrops shine—
  My heart *will* act so queerly.
She says, " My papa is so good,"
  Though I'm unworthy of her.
Dear little type of maidenhood,
  I love her, oh, I love her.

I think sometimes I'd like to go
  And tell her " I am sorry,"
For, oh, my feet do falter so
  'Mid life's unending worry.
Dear, loyal heart!   Suppose I should
  (I have done so—or nearly),
She'd only say, " My papa's good.
  I love him, oh, so dearly."

So, 'mid the storm of life and years,
  My little daughter's kisses
And loyal faith have dried my tears,
  And cares exchanged for blisses.
And, as I write, if tears will start,·
  They're tears of gladness merely,
For these words bless my weary heart:
  " I love my papa dearly."

WHEN I GO OUT ON MY WHEEL.

WHEN I go out on my wheel, the world
　　Goes scurrying past, as the Hand unfurled
The leagues of hurrying brown or green;
And I see the little white houses between
The hedges and trees, and the air strikes hard
On my lifted face, and the odor of nard,
Of myrtle and roses, exalts like wine,
As I ride on my wheel and the world is mine.

When I go out on my wheel, the town
Fades away—fades away into stretches of brown;
And I hear the murmur of brooks that run
Through the shady nooks till they greet the sun.
And it's ho! oho! for the joy I feel
As I ride, as I glide, on my steed of steel;
And the day and its moments are all divine,
As I ride on my wheel and the world is mine.

When I go out on my wheel, I know
That back to the toil and the grind I must go;
But I do not mind as the moments fly,
For the world is fair and its child am I.
So it's ho! for the hedges that glide and glide,
And it's ho! for the brooklets that hide and hide,
And it's ho! for the day with its smile benign,
When I ride on my wheel and the world is mine.

A SONG FOR THE RANK AND FILE.

NOT to the brave commanders who ordered
the boys to go
Where the hail of death beat on them and the
blood of the brave must flow;
Not to the ones who wore the straps, though
theirs is the hero's claim,
And their names and their deeds are written on
the wonderful scroll of Fame,
But to those, unsung, unhonored, who marched
at their country's call
Where lives went out to the battle shout and the
flag was a funeral pall;
To these, the humbler heroes, who marched
where their duty lay;
To the soldiers who bore the muskets, I'm singing a song to-day.

To the soldiers who bore the muskets—for them
    not a hope of fame,
Nor the witch'ry that lingers ever in that mys-
    tical spell, a name.
No dream of the future lured them, nor the heat
    of ambition's breath,
As they shouldered their muskets calmly and
    marched to the valley of death.
Where the Cuban suns beat on them, in the
    drench of the tropical rain,
Or stricken by Spanish bullets, they took up the
    burden of pain.
They saw but their duty, and did it—no hope of
    the laurel or bay,
And so to the boys with the muskets I'm sing-
    ing a song to-day.

The world has praise for its heroes, a chosen
    and honored few,
But I say that they all are heroes, the boys who
    have worn the blue.
They went at their country's summons; they of-
    fered their gift of life,
And what could the ones we honor do more in
    the nation's strife?
Unnamed in the "late dispatches," and weary
    and worn the while,
They marched where the bullets whistled, the
    men of the rank and file;
So others may chant their praises, the chosen
    and honored few,
I sing to the boys with the muskets—the men in
    the unstrapped blue.

HUSHABY, LULLABY.

HUSHABY, lullaby, my little men;
The sandman comes, but he goes again.
Hushaby, lullaby, little wee maids;
The round world turns and it seeks the shades,
And Sleep comes stealing adown, adown,
And he closes the eyes of blue or brown,
And he weaves his net and it holds you thrall—
Hushaby, lullaby, little ones all.

Hushaby, lullaby. One little star
Is peeping adown from afar, so far
That its great white light is a slender beam
When it reaches the world where the babies
    dream,
A slender beam that can only kiss
The little wee heads—for it came for this—
Ere it dies away in a glimmer small—
Hushaby, lullaby, little ones all.

Hushaby, lullaby. Life is a maze
Where blindly we wander through wearisome
days,
Through wearisome days when the spirit is
numb,
Till out of the shadows the little ones come.
Then mothers stoop to them to kiss and caress,
And the souls of the fathers they gladden and
bless;
For straight from the heavens God's angels they
call—
Hushaby, lullaby, little ones all.

IN OUR LAND OF CALIFORNIA.

W HEN the daylight all has faded and the
    sunbeams are at rest,
When the last faint streak of crimson dies to
    ashen in the west;
When the god of day and glory hides his face
    behind the world,
And the earth is like a maiden in a mantle dew-
    impearled,
Then beyond the untrod spaces, and beyond the
    misty bars,
In their distant, distant places shine the multi-
    tude of stars;
But their utmost, tender splendor, it is showered
    on us here,
In our land of California, in our Summer land
    of cheer.

There is glory in our sunlight as it sparkles o'er
    the plain,
As it laughs adown the valleys till the valleys
    laugh again;
But it's only when the starlight shimmers, glim-
    mers down the world
That back unto their hidden home the brood of
    trouble's hurled.
For who could harbor discontent when comfort's
    everywhere,
When peace is in the tranquil night and peace is
    in the air;
When every breeze that fans your cheek seems
    whispering, " Rest is here,"
In our land of California, in our Summer land
    of cheer.

That gray old mantle yonder, with its sparkling
    diamonds set,
Beyond its utmost border is the Land of Care
    and Fret;
And every star that sparkles there is where an
    angel stands,
And every breeze that whispers bears a blessing
    from His hands.
But in the Eastern country, lo! the mists are in
    the way,
And so the benediction's lost, the blessing goes
    astray;
But I think if man will listen he will hear that
    blessing here,
In our land of California, in our Summer land
    of cheer.

.

REACH DOWN FROM YOUR HEAVEN.

REACH down, reach down from your heaven,
    My love whom I loved so well,
For my day sinks down to its even,
    And the darkening shadows dwell
Where my heart like a monk is sitting
    Mid the wrack of its wasted years,
And my soul of its hopes is knitting
    A shroud that is bleached by tears.

Reach down, reach down from your heaven,
    For I dream in the mist-hid sphere,
The God to your soul hath given
    The right of returning here,
And, lo! when the twilight presses
    Its seal on my dreamy eyes,
You come with the old caresses,
    And care from my spirit flies.

They say, where the white rose blooming
  Smiles back to the smile of its God,
You lie in the daytime and glooming,
  Asleep 'neath the life-giving sod;
But I fathomed the lie that they told me
  When you came in the even's shade
To kiss and caress and enfold me,
  With your heart to my warm heart laid.

Then the years turned back in their creeping,
  And the past was again to-day,
And I knew that you waked from your sleeping
  To lighten the weary way
I walk through the tear-wet valley
  Which leads to the hills of light,
Where the angels of happiness rally
  And His smile breaks the seal of the night.

Reach down, reach down from your heaven,
  Lest my soul in its helplessness fall,
And I take of the world's dread leaven
  That poisons the spirit of all.
Then whisper me upward and onward,
  Though they tell me my dream is a lie;
For the soul that cleaves starward and sunward
  Shall live though the universe die.

THE POOR LITTLE BIRDIES.

THE poor little birdies that sleep in the trees,
    Going rockaby, rockaby, lulled by the
        breeze;
The poor little birdies, they make me feel bad,
Oh, terribly, dreadfully, dismally sad,
For—think of it, little one; ponder and weep—
The birdies must stand when they sleep, when
        they sleep;
            And their poor little legs—
                I am sure it is so—
                They ache, and they ache,
                    For they're weary, you know.
And that is the reason that far in the night
You may hear them say " Dear-r-r! " if you lis-
        ten just right,
For the poor little birdies would sleep on the
        bough,
And they want to lie down, but they do not
        know how.

Just think of it, darling; suppose you must stand
On those little brown legs, all so prettily
    planned;
Suppose you must stand when you wanted to
    sleep,
I am sure you would call for your mama and
    weep,
And your poor little legs, they would cramp, I
    have guessed,
And your poor little knees, they would call for a
    rest;
       And you'd cry, I am sure,
         For so weary you'd be;
       And you'd want to lie down,
         But you couldn't, you see.
And that is the reason why we should feel bad
For the poor little birdies, who ought to be glad;
For they want to lie down as they sleep on the
    bough;
They want to lie own, but they don't know
    how.

THE BROOK THAT RAN DOWN TO THE MILL.

I MET you that night at the charity ball,
  And you looked like a fairyland queen,
And your smile was so gracious it held me in
    thrall,
  A most willing captive, I ween;
And I wondered, I wondered—perhaps it was
    wrong—
  If then you remembered them still,
The days when we waded the afternoons long
  In the brook that ran down to the mill.

I am only a scribe, with a pencil for fate,
  While you are a fairyland queen,
But someway I thought as the moments grew
    late
  That perhaps you remembered that scene,
When two little children, with little bare legs,
  And voices with laughter athrill,
Dug deep in the sand for the brown turtle's
    eggs,
  Near the brook that ran down to the mill.

And I wondered, I wondered—perhaps it was
    wrong—
  If you wouldn't be willing, you know,
To wander again to that country of song
  Where the barefooted little ones go;
And I would go with you; my pencil should fall,
  And my fancy should rest at its will,
While with pin-hooks we'd fish for the "shiners"
    o'ersmall
  In the brook that ran down to the mill.

Oh, queen of the fairyland, little bare feet
  Are hardly a dress-party theme,
But, someway, to me is their memory sweet,
  As their patter I hear in my dream;
And—honest—whatever life's glories may be,
  Would you not barter all for the thrill
That you knew in the past when you waded with
    me
  In the brook that ran down to the mill?

AS WE JOG ON TOGETHER.

I LOVE my love, and she loves me.
　　We jog along together
O'er rocky upland, flowery lea,
　　Through fair or stormy weather.
And if the day bring naught of cheer,
　　Or if the way be weary,
'Tis all forgotten when she's near,
　　My dearie, oh, my dearie.

Sometimes the mists about us close,
　　Of doubt and boding blended,
And where we journey neither knows,
　　Nor where the journey's ended.
Yet do we but the closer press,
　　While fogs creep o'er the heather,
And still we feel that life doth bless,
　　As we jog on together.

A little homely home of cheer;
  Two hearts that love me dearly—
If this bring not a heaven here,
  I know it does it nearly.
So if the suns shall shine or hide,
  Be fair or foul the weather,
I'm full content the end to bide
  While we jog on together.

"MY BROTHER'LL BE ALL RIGHT."

I ALWAYS was in those old days the family's
   blackest sheep;
Somehow I couldn't curb the blood that in my
   veins would leap.
My cousins walked a straight-hewn path accord-
   ing to a rule,
And rarely swore, and never fought nor " hook-
   ey " played at school;
And all my uncles shook their heads and said,
   " He will go bad;
There never was more cussedness boiled down
   in one small lad."
But whatsoever they all vowed, and whatsoe'er
   my plight,
My sister stood right up and said, " My brother'll
   be all right."

She didn't say, " My brother *is*," you mind—
  she didn't dare;
But when she said, " My brother'll *be*," I'd vow
  right then and there
That though I fell and barked my shins until
  they were a sight,
I'd rise again and prove at last that that dear
  girl was right.
And so her trust would follow me, for boys, you
  know, like men,
Whene'er they fall need human faith to pick
  them up again;
And few I think are ever lost or conquered in
  the fight
Who somewhere know one soul that says, " My
  brother'll be all right."

Sometimes in that sweet hour before the daylight
    all had fled
My sister'd creep into my arms and rest her bon-
    nie head
Upon my shoulder, and she'd tell of all she
    dreamed for me.
Oh, loyal heart of foolish faith! Through cyes
    bedimmed I see
The eyes of blue her soul looked through, the
    face with love aglow,
And scarcely will my heart believe 'twas long, so
    long ago,
That golden hour; for still I hear as 'twere but
    yesternight
The words she whispered in my ear, "My
    brother'll be all right."

'Twas long ago; the frost of Time has cooled my
    youthful blood;
No more it hurries to and fro, nor runs a restless
    flood.
The miles are wide 'twixt her and me; the years
    are long between;
She walks where earth's asleep in white, and I
    where it is green;
Yet does her faith still urge me on, and whisper
    me, " Be true,"
To fight my fight, and, stumbling oft, the battle
    yet renew;
And I reply: Oh, sister mine, though dark may
    be the night,
I'll justify the trust that said, " My brother'll be
    all right."

KNEE-DEEP IN CLOVER.

KNEE-DEEP in clover the way I used to be,
When earth was more like Heaven than
    now it seems to me;
When the bees were droning 'round me as if
    they didn't care
To work too hard with laziness just pulsing in
    the air;
When skies were clear, so crystal clear that I
    could look up through
And sort of fancy that I saw the things the an-
    gels do;
        When far or near,
        And rising clear,
    The notes of birds fell on my ear;
With chipmunks sitting on the fence and talking
    back to me—
Knee-deep in clover the way I used to be.

Knee-deep in clover, with robins chirping
  'round,
And all the world about me just running o'er
  with sound;
Fellow whistling yonder merry as could be;
River dimpling in the sun as if 'twere wooing
  me;
Fragrance of the blossoms—nothing like it
  now—
Nature smiling on me as she's forgotten how;
      A dream of peace,
      To never cease
    Till life gives memory her release;
With gladness whispering in my heart and fill-
  ing, thrilling me—
Knee-deep in clover the way I used to be.

TENDERLY TAKE AND HOLD THEM.

THY strong right hand, O, my Father,
    Reach down and tenderly press
To the eyes where the teardrops gather;
    Reach down with a soft caress,
And through the dark night spaces
    Let dreams like the angels come,
To gladden with memory's graces
    The hearts by their pain made numb.

With eyes that are wistful and weary
    They look to the shadowy veil,
And still are the long hours dreary,
    And still do the visions fail.
Then come when the night's gray streamers
    Float back from the faded day,
And gladden the pale-faced dreamers
    And soothe all their trials away.

Where the chasms of life are yawning
  They struggle and falter and fall;
They stand with their eyes to the dawning,
  But darkness is over them all.
Then tenderly take and hold them,
  As mothers their babes caress;
In the arms of Thy pity enfold them,
  And soothe them, and comfort, and bless.

As the breeze to the toiler seemeth;
  As the dews to the heart of the rose;
As love to the maiden that dreameth;
  As the rains that the desert knows,
So come when the world lies sleeping,
  Soft rocked in the cradle of rest,
Thy loved in Thy strong arms keeping
  Close, close to Thine infinite breast.

WHEN THE OLD MAN DREAMED.

SOMETIMES 'long after supper my grand-
      sire used to sit
Where the sunbeams through the window things
      of beauty liked to knit,
And he'd light his pipe and sit there in a sort of
      waking dream,
While to bathe his form in glory seemed the sun-
      light's pretty scheme;
And then, whatever happened, he didn't seem to
      see,
And a smile lit up his features that used to puzzle
      me,
And I would often wonder what pleasant inner
      theme
Had caused that strange and tranquil smile when
      grandpa used to dream.

Sometimes, though, when I'd listen I'd hear the
    good man sigh,
And once I'm almost sure I saw the moisture in
    his eye,
But whether he would smile or sigh, he didn't
    seem to see
The things that happened 'round him, and that's
    what puzzled me.
With the wreaths of smoke ascending as the twi-
    light gathered there,
The shadows crept about him in the old arm-
    chair,
And through the evening darkness I could see
    the fitful gleam
From the embers in his lighted pipe when grand-
    pa used to dream.

I used to wonder in those days. I wonder now
    no more,
For now I understand the thing that puzzled me
    of yore,
And I know that through the twilight and the
    shadows gathering fast
Came unto my grandsire, dreaming, the visions
    of the past.
The boys who played with him were there within
    that little room;
His mother's smile no doubt lit up the darkness
    and the gloom;
Again he ran and leaped and played beside an
    Eastern stream;
The ones he loved were there, I know, when
    grandpa used to dream.

And so he smiled—and then she stood, his dear-
    est, at his side,
With the glow of youth upon her, red-lipped and
    laughing-eyed,
And he told the old, sweet story, and she lis-
    tened, nothing loth,
And dreams of hope were written in the happy
    hearts of both;
And then, by strange transition, he saw her
    pulseless lie—
And 'twas then I viewed the moisture in the cor-
    ner of his eye.
Old friends were gathered round him, though
    they'd crossed death's mystic stream,
In that hour of smiles and sighing when my
    grandsire used to dream.

Oh, glad, sad gift of memory to call our dear
    ones back
And win them from their narrow homes to
    Time's still beaten track!
Yours was the power my grandsire held while
    twilight turned to night;
Through you his loved returned again and
    blessed his longing sight;
And I no longer wonder, when his dreaming I
    recall,
At smiles and sighs succeeding while the shad-
    ows hid us all,
For, while my pencil's trailing and I've half for-
    got my theme,
I, too, am seeing visions, as my grandsire used
    to dream.

"I'M PRAYING FOR YOU."

THERE'S a quaint little letter that lies on
   my stand,
A quaint little letter in old-fashioned hand.
It is lacking somewhat in rhetorical grace,
And its capital letters at times lose their place;
It scarcely would bear the most critical test,
Yet of all correspondence I hold it the best,
For it ends—ah, in love it was written all
   through:
" Remember, my boy, that I'm praying for you."

" Remember, my boy "—oh, an old boy am I,
With a head that shines back to the laugh of the
   sky,
But to her I'm " my boy," and I always will be,
Till the white angel steps 'twixt my mother and
   me,
And longer—the love that has guarded my way
I know will not cease at the close of the day,
But will whisper me still from the infinite blue,
" Remember, my boy, that I'm praying for you."

" I'm praying for you "—God knows we all need
That some heart of love to the Father shall plead,
For our feet will but stumble on life's rugged
      way,
And we frequently find that we're sadly astray.
We say to our spirits, " Be brave and press on,"
But the spirit will faint and the soul will grow
      wan;
And then comes the message, our strength to
      renew:
" Remember, my boy, that I'm praying for you."

Remember! Oh, mother, I could not forget.
Still the dear, loving message my lashes will wet,
As I read it here written in old-fashioned hand
In the quaint little letter that lies on my stand;
And in fancy I see you, as often of old,
When love kissed your face into beauty untold,
As you knelt by my cot—With eyes strangely
      dim,
Your boy *does* remember you're praying for him.

THE OLD, OLD SONG.

HERE is a song that no one sings;
   Here are the words that no one knows.
Out of the breath of a thousand springs,
   Out of the chill of a thousand snows,
Cometh the song that I sing to-day,
A song that is new and is old alway:

   A little joy, a little woe,
   An unseen path we blindly go,
  A little time for weeping,
   A little hour to walk or creep,
   A little faith but half to keep—
And then there comes the sleeping.

A song that echoes down the years;
  A song as old as time is old;
A song we hear with falling tears,
  While heads turn gray and hearts grow cold;
The old, old song, the song of life,
A chant from out a vale of strife:

  A little joy, a little woe,
  An unseen path we blindly go,
A little time for weeping,
  A little hour to walk or creep,
  A little faith but half to keep—
And then the **final** sleeping.